Blow Me a Kiss

Karen Collum · Serena Geddes

Sandy Creek
NEW YORK

SANDY CREEK and the distinctive Sandy Creek logo are registered trademarks of Barnes & Noble, Inc.

Text © 2010 by Karen Collum
Illustrations © 2010 by Serena Geddes

This 2012 custom edition is published exclusively for Sandy Creek by New Frontier Publishing.

Designed by Nicholas Pike

ISBN 978-1-4351-4513-9 (hbk.)

National Library of Australia Cataloging-in-Publication entry

Author: Collum, Karen.
Title: Blow Me a Kiss
written by Karen Collum; illustrated by Serena Geddes.
Edition: 1st ed.
Target Audience: For pre-school age.
Subjects: Kissing--Juvenile fiction.
Other Authors/Contributors: Geddes, Serena.

Dewey Number: A823.4

Manufactured in China
Lot #:
2 4 6 8 10 9 7 5 3
01/15

For Samuel. I love you to heaven and back.
KC

To Brayden, Nyah, Kyan, Lauren, Justin, Flynn,
Lana and Clayton for all your loving kisses.
From Aunty Reeni.
SG

Samuel was excited.
It was shopping day.

He loved going shopping with Mommy.

Samuel smiled at a lady in the post office,
but she didn't smile back.

She kept looking at her watch
and tapping her toes.

Samuel blew her a kiss.

It flew under the table,

over the greeting cards,

between the envelopes,

around her legs, and landed on her cheek with a loud 'SPLAT!'

The lady gasped and felt her face.

She stopped looking at her watch
and tapping her toes.

Instead, she played peek-a-boo
until they reached the front of the line.

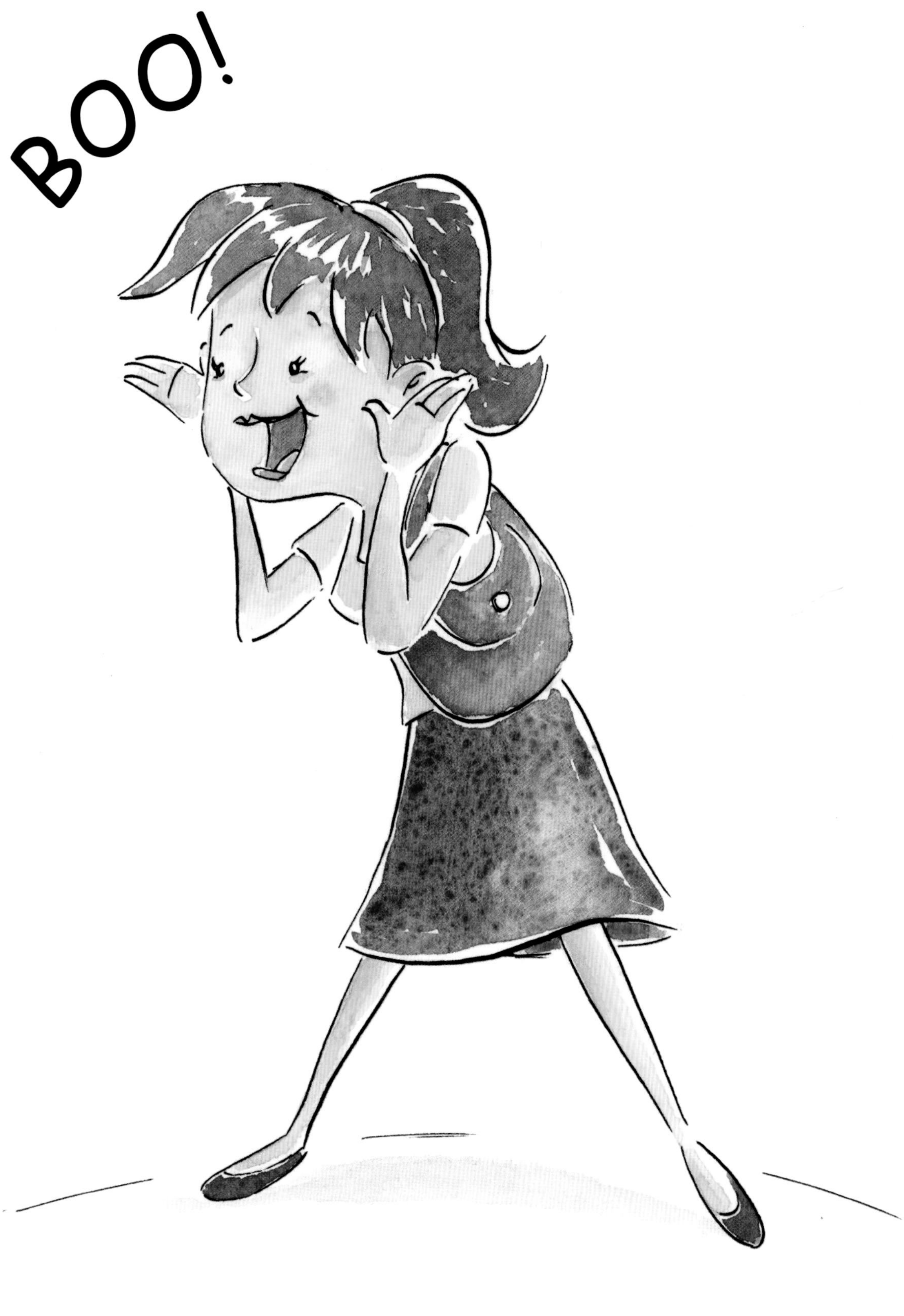
BOO!

In the supermarket Samuel helped Mommy search
for apples and avocados, bananas and lettuce,
and carrots and chocolate cake.

Samuel smiled at the shopkeeper arranging oranges,
but she didn't smile back.

Her shoulders were droopy and her feet were heavy.

Samuel blew her a kiss.

It flew through the donuts,

over the apples,

around the watermelon,

between the pineapples,

and landed on her forehead
with a loud 'SPLAT!'

The shopkeeper jumped
and felt her face.

Her shoulders weren't droopy anymore
and her feet weren't heavy.
Instead, she picked up three oranges and juggled.

Samuel and Mommy then went to the bank,
where he saw an old man waiting.
Samuel gave him a smile.

The old man didn't smile back.
He leaned heavily on his walking stick
and rubbed his aching hip.

Samuel blew him a kiss.

It flew under the chair,

behind the poster,

over the counter,

between the tellers, and landed on his nose with a loud 'SPLAT!'

The old man yelped and felt his face.

He didn't rub his aching hip or lean
on his walking stick anymore.
Instead, he danced a little jig.

It wasn't long before Samuel's kisses filled the shopping center.

Finally, it was time to go home.
Mommy smiled at Samuel as she put him in the car.

Samuel rubbed his eyes and yawned a big yawn.

Mommy blew Samuel a gentle kiss.

It floated over the steering wheel,
under the seatbelt, around the flowers,
over the groceries, behind the seat,

around the purple elephant,
under the toy truck,
swept past the cuddly lion ...

and landed on his soft,
rosy cheek without a sound.